A NOTE TO PARENTS AND CAREGIVERS

The diagnosis of cancer in a young child i
Children worry about what's going on in th
will affect their lives. Parents worry about
the treatment options. Caregivers do their
struggle to talk with their children about cancer, but misunderstand-
ing, denial, and apprehension often distort the communication process.
Frustration and fear can build up as parents respond to their child's
curiosity with hesitation. Parents must provide appropriate information
about cancer to gain the confidence they need to do the best they can for
their child.

As an oncologist who specializes in treating women and children,
I have discussed the diagnosis of cancer with many children. I have
answered the hard questions posed by children and their parents, and I
have learned how the right response can help the healing process.

I wrote this book to help parents and caregivers answer the questions most commonly asked by children with cancer. In my experience,
a diagnosis of cancer can so overwhelm parents that they lose the ability
to communicate effectively with their children. All too often parents
and caregivers give children different messages about the disease and its
possible treatments. My hope is that this book will help guide parents,
children, and caregivers as they search for appropriate answers to questions about cancer and develop a common understanding of the challenges facing them.

Please read this book together with your child or your patient. Let
him or her look through the book alone. Respond to any additional
questions that arise. And always project a positive and open attitude.
Together, you and your child or patient will conquer the Worry Wombat
and calmly face the challenges of dealing with cancer.

—M. Maitland DeLand, M.D.

This book is dedicated to Macie Landry,
the bravest and funniest child I know. —M.D.

Published by Greenleaf Book Group Press
Austin, Texas
www.gbgpress.com

Distributed by Greenleaf Book Group LLC

For ordering information or special discounts for bulk purchases, please contact
Greenleaf Book Group LLC at PO Box 91869, Austin, TX 78709, 512.891.6100.

Design and composition by Greenleaf Book Group LLC
Cover design by Greenleaf Book Group LLC
Illustrations by Jennifer Zivoin

Publisher's Cataloging-In-Publication Data (Prepared by The Donohue Group, Inc.)

DeLand, M. Maitland.
The Great Katie Kate. Tackles questions about cancer / M. Maitland
DeLand ; with illustrations by Jennifer Zivoin. -- 1st ed.
p. : ill. ; cm.

Summary: A book that follows a superhero figure (the Great Katie Kate) as she
explains to a young girl what is happening when she is diagnosed with cancer.
Interest age level: 004-006.
ISBN: 978-1-60832-027-1

1. Cancer in children--Treatment--Juvenile fiction. 2. Cancer--Patients--Juvenile fiction. 3.
Children--Preparation for medical care--Juvenile fiction. 4. Superheroes--Juvenile fiction. 5.
Cancer in children--Treatment--Fiction. 6. Cancer--Patients--Fiction. 7. Medical care--Fiction. 8.
Superheroes--Fiction. I. Zivoin, Jennifer. II. Title. III. Title: Tackles questions about cancer

PZ7.D37314 Gr 2010
[E]   2009942924

Part of the Tree Neutral™ program, which offsets the number of trees consumed in
the production and printing of this book by taking proactive steps, such as planting
trees in direct proportion to the number of trees used: www.treeneutral.com.

TreeNeutral

Manufactured by Shanghai iPrinting Co., Ltd on acid-free paper
Manufactured in Shanghai, China. March 2010
Batch No. 1

10 11 12 13 14   10 9 8 7 6 5 4 3 2 1
First Edition

THE Great Katie Kate

TACKLES QUESTIONS ABOUT CANCER

M. Maitland DeLand, M.D.

with illustrations by Jennifer Zivoin

GREENLEAF
BOOK GROUP PRESS

Suzy was not feeling well. She had a lump on her leg, which did not go away after her pediatrician gave her several weeks of antibiotics. Her pediatrician wasn't sure what was wrong, so Suzy and her parents went to see a special doctor, Dr. DeMarco.

"I believe that your daughter may have cancer," Dr. DeMarco told Suzy's parents. "We will have to perform certain tests so that we can be sure. Then we can discuss treatment. The nurse has some forms for you to sign. I'll wait here with Suzy."

"Don't worry," said her daddy. "We'll be right back."

But Suzy *did* begin to worry. "Cancer? Tests? What's going to happen to me?"

"I've got a friend who can help, Suzy," said Dr. DeMarco.

A bright streak of light zoomed through the window, and with a flash, a young girl with a cape stood in the examining room.

"Who are you?" Suzy asked.

"I'm the Great Katie Kate. It sounds like you have a whole bunch of questions. I'm going to answer them while Dr. DeMarco talks with your parents."

"See you later, Suzy," said Dr. DeMarco.

"But—" Suzy said. She was very worried.

Just then, a large, furry critter appeared. It looked sad and worried, just like Suzy.

"Uh-oh," Katie Kate said. "I see the Worry Wombat."

"The Worry Wombat?" asked Suzy.

"The Worry Wombat is my name," it said with a sniffle, "and causing worries is my game."

"I don't think I like the Worry Wombat," Suzy whispered.

"Don't be afraid of the Worry Wombat, Suzy. If you ask enough questions and smile whenever you can, the Worry Wombat will shrink and disappear."

Suzy got up the courage to ask, "Dr. DeMarco says I might have cancer, Katie Kate. What does that mean?"

Katie Kate smiled. "Come with me and I'll explain."

"Cancer is something that grows in your body and makes you sick," Katie Kate said.

"Like this lump on my leg?" Suzy asked. "I took medicine for four weeks, and it still didn't go away."

"That lump might be cancer. Dr. DeMarco won't know until she performs some tests. The first one is a biopsy."

"A biopsy? Will that hurt?"

"Just a little pinch. The doctor just performed a biopsy on that girl. She gave her a shot with some medicine to make sure she wouldn't feel anything. Then Dr. DeMarco took out a little piece of the lump and looked at it under a microscope to see if she had cancer. A special doctor called a pathologist will also analyze the biopsy tissues."

"That girl sure has a pretty Band-aid," Suzy said. "I can't wait to get a pretty Band-aid, too. I'm not worried about the biopsy anymore."

Katie Kate congratulated her. "Brave girl! Look, you've made the Worry Wombat start to shrink."

"What other tests do I have to take, Katie Kate? I got an A on my spelling test last week and it was hard."

"These tests are a little different. You won't have to work hard; you'll just have to follow instructions. The next test will probably be an X-ray. A doctor will use a special machine to take pictures."

"Mommy and Daddy took lots of pictures at my birthday party."

"Wasn't that fun! Those were pictures of how you look on the outside. The X-ray machine takes pictures of how you look on the inside. This boy is getting an X-ray of his leg. Can you see what he looks like on the inside?"

"Does it hurt to have an X-ray?"

"No, it doesn't," Katie Kate explained. "But you have to stay very, very still while they take the picture. Your parents will watch through a window."

"That's good," Suzy said. "I'm not worried about the X-ray anymore." And Suzy gave Katie Kate a small smile.

"That's the way, Suzy," Katie Kate said. And the Worry Wombat shrunk a little more.

"You might have some other tests,
Suzy, like a CT scan, which is a
special kind of X-ray."

11

"Or a blood test. The doctor might need to look at your blood under a microscope to see why you are feeling bad."

"Will the blood test hurt?" Suzy asked.

"It will feel like a pinch, and then the hurt will go away."

"I'm not afraid of these tests anymore," Suzy announced.
And the Worry Wombat shrunk again.

"Some kids have to stay in the hospital when they're sick, right? I've never stayed in a hospital before."

"You have stayed in a hospital, Suzy. You were born in a hospital, so you stayed there when you were a little baby."

"But why might I have to stay in the hospital now?"

"So that everyone can take good care of you."

"Will I have to stay all by myself?"

"Oh, no. This girl isn't by herself. Her mother, father, and friends are all visiting her. And your family can come to visit you, too, when you stay in the hospital."

"What will they give me to eat?"

"Anything you want."

"Even yellow jello?"

"Yes, even yellow jello. Just tell the nurse what you want and she will bring it to you. Everyone wants to help you, Suzy. They all care about you."

"Katie Kate, I heard Dr. DeMarco say the word *surgery*. What is it?"

"Surgery is a procedure that will help you feel much better, Suzy."

"I remember when Grandma had something wrong in her tummy. She went to the hospital and had surgery. Then she came home and her tummy hurt a little, but she got a lot better. Will I have to have surgery?"

"Dr. DeMarco will look at all your tests and then she will decide. Surgery always takes place in a special room in the hospital, and there are special doctors who work hard to make you well."

"Does surgery hurt?"

"No. You will be asleep the whole time, and then you will wake up in the recovery room, just like this girl here."

"I won't worry about surgery anymore."

And what happened to the Worry Wombat?

"Katie Kate, what else might happen in the hospital?"
"The doctor might want you to have chemotherapy. Chemotherapy medicines are special medicines that help make cancer go away. These children are having chemotherapy."

"What are those tubes?"

"The medicines flow through the tubes into your body."

"Does chemotherapy hurt?"

"When you first sit down, you will feel a needle prick your arm. Or a special receptor might be placed in your chest so that chemotherapy is always easy to receive. It might not be very comfortable, but it won't hurt for long. Your mommy and daddy can even sit beside you and read you stories while you are getting the medicine. Sometimes after you get the medicine you feel tired, and sometimes you get a tummy ache. These are called side effects. But the doctor will give you medicine for them."

Katie Kate said, "Sometimes chemotherapy medicine can make your hair fall out."

"Do you mean I won't have my blonde hair?"

"Maybe, but maybe not. But your beautiful blonde hair will grow back. In the meantime, you can wear all kinds of hats and wigs, just like these kids."

"I like wearing baseball caps," Suzy said. "That boy said he was going to have radiation therapy. What's that?"

"Take my hand; I'll show you."

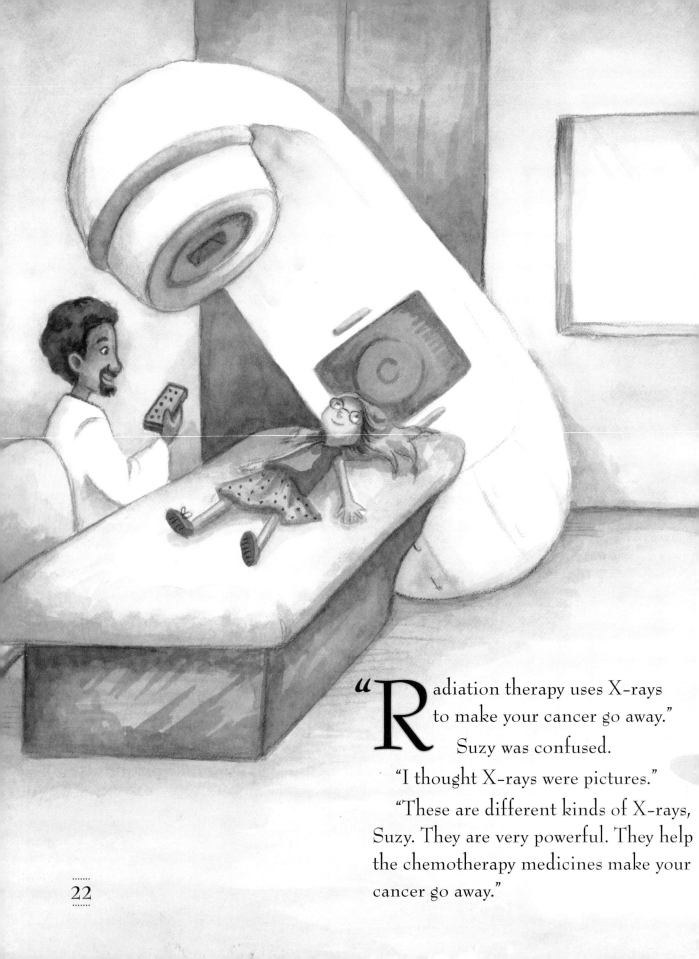

"Radiation therapy uses X-rays to make your cancer go away."
Suzy was confused.
"I thought X-rays were pictures."
"These are different kinds of X-rays, Suzy. They are very powerful. They help the chemotherapy medicines make your cancer go away."

22

"Does radiation therapy hurt?"

"Oh, no, it doesn't hurt at all. But while you are getting your radiation therapy, you have to hold very, very still, just like this girl. And there are her mommy and daddy."

"I'm not worried about radiation therapy, Katie Kate."

"And look at how small the Worry Wombat is, Suzy."

"Well, Suzy, do you have any more questions?"

"No," Suzy said with a big smile. "Thanks, Katie Kate. I won't worry anymore."

Suzy looked around the room. "Where is the Worry Wombat?"

"You made the Worry Wombat disappear. Great job!"

"Will he come back?"

"As long as you ask questions and keep smiling, Suzy, the Worry Wombat will never return. And now it's time for me to go away."

"But—"

"Remember, if you have any questions, just ask. Good-bye, Suzy!"

"Good-bye, Katie Kate!"

The Great Katie Kate zoomed out of the window just as Suzy's parents entered the examination room.

"Mommy, Daddy, the Great Katie Kate came to help me and she answered all my questions and flew me around the hospital, and—"

"Katie Kate?" Suzy's mommy asked.
"What are you talking about?"

"I know just what Suzy's talking about," Dr. DeMarco said. "The Great Katie Kate is famous around here. Did she help answer your questions, Suzy?"

"Yes, she did. And I made the Worry Wombat disappear."

"You're a very brave girl, Suzy."

The End.